E   11615

AUSTIN, MARGOT

Peter Churchmouse

8-63

NOV 8 1966 -241 MAY 2 1 1985
AP 25 67 -283
                              11615

E
DATE DUE   Austin - Peter churchmouse

APR 1 1982				
FEB 2 1 1984				
MAY 2 1 1985				
JUL 2 1987				
SEP 2 4 1987				
JE 27 '96				

DEMCO 25-370

PETER CHURCHMOUSE

Written and Illustrated

BY MARGOT AUSTIN

1941

E. P. DUTTON AND COMPANY, INC.

New York

PETER CHURCHMOUSE

S - N - A - P! went the snap-rat.

PETER CHURCHMOUSE

Up jumped Peter!
S-N-A-P! went the snap-rat!
Poor little Peter Churchmouse raised his eyebrows
the way he always did when he made a poem,

> "I wish the cheese I ate
> Were on a plate
> That wouldn't snap at me
> Because I DON'T LIKE IT!"

Then Peter sat right down on the big wooden snap-
rat and ate his cheese. Every last bit.

"Now," said Peter, "I shall bite another big hole in
something so that Parson Pease-Porridge will put more
cheese on the snap-rat for tomorrow."

So Peter ate a great big hole in the red felt that lined
Parson Pease-Porridge's best collection basket.

"There," said Peter, "Parson Pease-Porridge will be
sure to notice that!"

"I'll be twitched," said Parson Pease-Porridge next morning when he saw the great big hole that Peter had made in the best collection basket.

"These holes will be the ruination of me. I must do something drastic! I'll show these rats—I'll get a *cat!!*"

"Oh-h-h," said Peter Churchmouse. "Oh-h-h, poor me!"

Then Peter Churchmouse raised his eyebrows the way he always did when he thought of a poem,

>"I believe I heard
>That terrible word
>I'm scared to tell it
>So I'll only spell it—
>C-A-T!"

Next day Peter looked for cheese on the snap-rat as usual.

But the snap-rat was gone and in its place was a bowl of milk. And beside the bowl of milk was Gabriel.

"Hello," said Peter stepping bravely from behind the organ, "I'm afraid of cats. Are you a cat?"

"Who? Me?" said Gabriel sitting up, "I'm not a cat. I'm a kitten and my name's Gabriel. Are you a rat?"

"Of course not," said Peter. "I'm a poor Church-mouse and my name is Peter."

"Hello, Peter," said Gabriel. "I'm to scare the rats away. The rats who've been eating big holes in things. Do you know how to scare rats?"

"No I don't," said Peter. "And if I did it wouldn't help you because there aren't any rats here at all. There's only poor me. I pretend I'm rats. *I* bite the great big holes in everything!"

"You don't!" said Gabriel.

"I do," said Peter. "Once I even ate a hymn book. It tasted awful."

"For pity's sake," said Gabriel in a shocked voice. "Cover and all?"

"Cover and all," said Peter. "And I didn't like to do it."

"Then why *did* you do it?" asked Gabriel.

"Because I was hungry," said Peter. "I'm *always* hungry!"

"How sad for you," said Gabriel. "Parson Pease-Porridge gives *me* lots to eat."

"That's because you're a big kitten and he can see you," cried poor Peter. "But I'm a little mouse and he can't see me at all. He's too near-sighted! He doesn't even know I live here. And now that you've come even the snap-rat is gone. All I ever got to eat was the cheese on the snap-rat and I wouldn't have got that if Parson Pease-Porridge didn't think I was the rats that make the holes *I* bite in things. Fuss, fuss, fuss. Oh, I don't like it!"

"How very sad," said Gabriel. "How very, very sad."

"Sad indeed," said Peter, "I even make poems about it."

"I'd like to hear one, please," said Gabriel.

"Gladly," said Peter, raising his eyebrows. "One goes like this—

Snap, whack, bang,
Goes the snap-rat bang,
Goes snap bang,
Goes whack bang,
Fuss, fuss, fuss!"

"It's a beautiful poem," said Gabriel admiringly. "I could listen and listen and listen."

"Thank you kindly," said Peter.

"Maybe I can help you think of a way to let Parson Pease-Porridge know he has a poor hungry Churchmouse," said Gabriel. "So you'll get lots to eat like I do."

"But how?" said Peter.

"I really don't know," said Gabriel. "I'll think very hard."

"Please do," said Peter. "Think hard while I have a lick of your milk."

So Peter played hide-behind-the-hymn-book on the shelf where the hymn books were kept. And Gabriel played chew-the-toe with Parson Pease-Porridge's old black slipper. And they both played slide-up-and-down the pew bench.

And all the while Peter longed and longed for cheese. And all the while Gabriel thought and thought about how he could help poor Peter. But Gabriel couldn't think of a single way.

"Listen, Gabriel," said Peter at last.

"I am," said Gabriel. "I'm listening."

"That's fine," said Peter, "Because *I* have an idea about how I can get Parson Pease-Porridge to notice me."

"And get some cheese," added Gabriel.

"Well," said Peter. "I've heard Parson Pease-Porridge say that little children who drink lots of milk grow up to be big children, and you're a big kitten so it must be because you drink lots of milk. So *maybe* if I drink lots of milk I'll grow so big that Parson Pease-Porridge will be able to see me!"

"I *am* a big kitten," admitted Gabriel. "So that must be the reason. Help yourself to some more of my milk."

"Thank you," said Peter between licks, "I much pre-fer cheese but I'll take anything, even milk, if only Parson Pease-Porridge will notice me!"

"I'll be twitched," remarked Parson Pease-Porridge. "I never knew a kitten to drink so much milk!"

For Peter drank and drank and drank Gabriel's milk every day. And every day he asked Gabriel if he had grown any bigger. And every day he looked in the mirror over the organ to see if he looked any bigger. And every day Gabriel measured him alongside Parson Pease-Porridge's ink bottle to see if he stretched any bigger—but he didn't. Not one bit.

"Except," said Gabriel, "your waist is nearly as round as the ink bottle."

"It's no use," said poor Peter, "no use at all."

"Make a poem about it," said Gabriel.

"Very well," said Peter, lifting his eyebrows—

> "Drink, drink, drink,
> To make me bigger;
> But all I do
> Is lose my figure.
> Fuss, fuss, fuss!"

"How beautiful," said Gabriel. "I could listen and listen."

Peter stopped dancing on the black notes of the organ and looked over the edge of the keyboard at Gabriel.

"Gabriel, do you know what?" asked Peter.

Gabriel stopped sharpening his nails on the organ's green carpet pedals and looked up at Peter.

"I don't," said Gabriel.

"I have another idea, that's what!" said Peter. "About how I can get Parson Pease-Porridge to notice me."

"And get some cheese," added Gabriel.

"If," said Peter, waving his arms, "Parson Pease-Porridge saw my nice red knitted bed he'd know it was much too small for rats to sleep in. So he'd know right off that a little Churchmouse slept in it. Wouldn't he?"

"Quite true," agreed Gabriel. "And it's such a beautiful bed, too."

"It *is* a nice bed," said Peter. "We'll put it beside his black leather book so he'll be sure to see it."

"We'll do it right now," said Gabriel, "because I've heard Parson Pease-Porridge say 'never put off till tomorrow what you can do right now.'"

So Peter and Gabriel laid the red knitted bed right beside the big black leather book.

"There," said Peter, "Parson Pease-Porridge will be *sure* to notice that!"

"I'll be twitched," said Parson Pease-Porridge when he saw Peter's knitted bed beside his black leather book.

"How in the world did my old red mitten get here? I've been hunting for that good red mitten for ages. Hem-mmp! I'm a forgetful old man! So I'll just put this mitten in my pocket so I won't lose it again, Hemp, hemp-p-p!"

And away went Parson Pease-Porridge with Peter's bed.

"How very, very sad," said Gabriel. "Now your bed's gone."

"It's the only bed I had," said poor little Peter. "The only bed I *ever* had."

"You *should* make a poem about it," encouraged Gabriel.

"I will," said Peter lifting his eyebrows—

"I had a bed,
My bed was red.
Now it's gone,
I have no place to rest my head.
It's gone—my lovely bed!"

"It's a beautiful poem," said Gabriel. "It's so sad, I could listen and listen and listen."

"Peter, do you know what?" asked Gabriel.

"I do not," said Peter who was sniffing the flowers that stood on Parson Pease-Porridge's desk.

"I have an idea," answered Gabriel, "that will be *sure* to get Parson Pease-Porridge to notice you."

"So I'll get some cheese," said Peter. "Hurry and tell me."

"It's this," said Gabriel. "If you stood right under Parson Pease-Porridge's nose he'd have to see you. Wouldn't he?"

"True," said Peter. "But how *can* I stand right under Parson Pease-Porridge's nose? He's much too tall."

"It's really quite simple," said Gabriel. "When Parson Pease-Porridge sits at his desk to read his big black book it's right under his nose. So if you jump out of those flowers, plop, onto the big black book you'll be right under his nose, too. Then if you'll stand very still he'll be sure to notice you."

"True, true," said Peter. "I'll climb into the flowers right now."

"Do hurry," whispered Gabriel. "Parson Pease-Porridge is coming!"

"Hum-mp," said Parson Pease-Porridge sitting down at his desk.

"Hemp, hem-mmp," said Parson Pease-Porridge opening his big black leather book.

"Now," whispered Peter to himself. "Now is the time!"

So plop, jumped Peter, plump in the middle. Right under Parson Pease-Porridge's nose!

"And *now*," said Peter to himself, "Parson Pease-Porridge will be *sure* to notice me."

"I'll be twitched," said Parson Pease-Porridge, pushing up his spectacles. "What's this? Oh, I'm a bothered old man.

"I'll be twitched," said Parson Pease-Porridge, pushing his spectacles down again. "I see a grey spot before my eyes!

"I must have my glasses changed," said he, closing his big book with a terrible—

B—A—N—G!

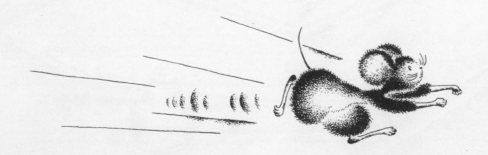

"Oh-h-h," gasped Peter. "Oh-h, poor me."

"He thought you were a grey spot," said Gabriel.

"I might have been," said Peter.

"Very true," said Gabriel. "How awful!"

"I shall make a poem about it," said Peter raising his eyebrows—

> "I jumped quick
> When the book closed whang.
> I learned the trick
> On the snap-rat bang.
> Fuss, fuss, fuss!"

"Very lovely," sighed Gabriel. "I could listen and listen."

"I have another idea," said Gabriel.

"About how I can get Parson Pease-Porridge to notice me so I'll get cheese?" asked Peter.

"That's right," said Gabriel.

"Then please stop playing jump-over-the-pew-bench," said Peter, "because I'm listening."

"It's this," said Gabriel. "I'll spill Parson Pease-Porridge's ink bottle. Then you can walk in the ink and make foot-prints on his big white blotter, and when he sees your little foot-prints he'll know you're a little Churchmouse."

"Then I'll get cheese," said Peter. "Cheese!"

"Quite true," said Gabriel. "Follow me."

So up they jumped onto Parson Pease-Porridge's desk. Gabriel gave the ink bottle a big push. Over it went and out came the ink.

"Now," said Gabriel. "Make some tracks."

"I will," said Peter running right through the ink and right onto Parson Pease-Porridge's clean white blotter. And he went round and round and round.

"Stop, Peter!" cried Gabriel. "Stop!"

"Why?" asked Peter.

"Because," cried Gabriel, "look what's happening!"

For every step poor Peter took on the blotter was spreading bigger and bigger.

"Don't make more prints. Parson Pease-Porridge will think I've done it," cried Gabriel. "Quick! Dry your feet on something!"

"I'll dry my feet here," said Peter, jumping from the blotter to the sermon that Parson Pease-Porridge had finished writing that very morning.

"Hurry, hurry," cried Gabriel. "Here comes Parson Pease-Porridge. We'd better go!"

"Fuss, fuss, fuss," said Peter wiping his feet very hard all along the bottom of Parson Pease-Porridge's sermon.

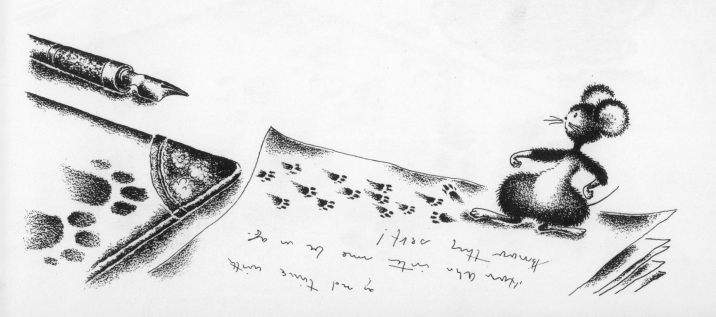

"I'll be twitched," said Parson Pease-Porridge, "Gabriel has spilled my ink! Tut, tut, look at his big tracks on my blotter!

"Tut, tut, *tut,*" said Parson Pease-Porridge looking from the blotter to his sermon, "I'm a bothered old man. It seems I've made foot-notes on the bottom of my sermon, but I can't seem to read them. Hem-mp! That settles it. I *must* have my glasses changed this *very* day.

"A pretty pass!" said Parson Pease-Porridge as he hurried away. "Can't even read my *own* foot-notes!"

"It's no use," said Peter. "Parson Pease-Porridge will never notice me. Never."

"And you'll never get any cheese," added Gabriel.

"But I *must* have cheese," cried Peter.

"How sad for you," said Gabriel. "Make a poem about it."

"I shall," said Peter lifting his eyebrows—

> "Oh, please, please,
> I want cheese.
> I'm sad, sad,
> I wish I had
> Cheese, Cheese, CHEESE!"

"Lovely," said Gabriel. "I could listen and listen."

"Gabriel," said Peter, "I'm going to bite a hole in something!"

"Oh, do!" encouraged Gabriel. "Do bite something!"

"I will," said Peter. "I'll bite a hole right through the middle of Parson Pease-Porridge's sermon! Then he'll notice me!"

So Peter began to bite and bite right through the middle of Parson Pease-Porridge's sermon.

"Oh my, it's the biggest hole I've ever seen," admired Gabriel, when Peter had finished.

"It's the biggest hole I ever bit," said Peter.

The next day Parson Pease-Porridge had a new pair of spectacles that were three times as thick and three times as strong as his old ones.

"Hem-mp," said he. "It's fine to have new spectacles. I can see everything. I believe I'll have a look at my sermon!

"I'll be twitched," cried Parson Pease-Porridge when he saw the *tremendous* hole in the middle of his sermon. "Oh ruination! Oh, I'm a bothered old man!"

And *then* Parson Pease-Porridge looked at the foot-notes that he couldn't read the day before.

"Upon my soul," cried Parson Pease-Porridge. "These are *not* foot-notes, these are foot-prints! Little foot-prints! I have a Churchmouse! Poor little thing he's eaten all these holes to show me he's hungry!"

"Hem-m-mp," said Parson Pease-Porridge. "Owing to this slight accident (here Parson Pease-Porridge looked at the hole in his sermon) I must abandon the text I prepared for today. So I shall speak about KIND-NESS instead. KINDNESS to very little animals.

"And now," smiled Parson Pease-Porridge, "never put off till tomorrow what you can do right now!

"I must get CHEESE for my Churchmouse!"

"Oh-h, Gabriel," whispered Peter. "Did you hear that?"

"I did," said Gabriel. "Parson Pease-Porridge has noticed you at last!"

"Oh, poor me," cried Peter. "I'm going to get cheese after all!"

"Quite true," replied Gabriel.

"I'll make a little poem about it," said Peter lifting his eyebrows the way he always did—

> "Cheese,
> Cheese, cheese,
> Cheese, cheese, cheese,
> C—H—E—E—S—E !"

"How beautiful," sighed Gabriel. "I could listen and listen and listen."

THE END

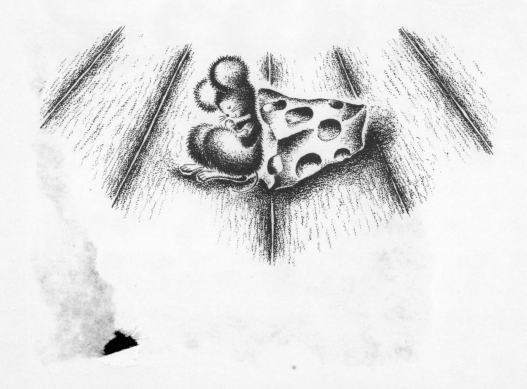